BAD KiTTY

MEETS THE
BABY

NICK BRUEL

ROARING BROOK PRESS
NEW YORK

For Emma, Isaac,
Lila, Will,
and Isabel

Published by Roaring Brook Press

Roaring Brook Press is a division of Holtzbrinck Publishing Holdings Limited Partnership

120 Broadway, New York, NY 10271 • mackids.com

Library of Congress Cataloging-in-Publication Data

Bruel, Nick.

Bad kitty meets the baby / Nick Bruel.

p. cm.

"A Neal Porter Book."

Summary: Bad kitty is not pleased when a baby joins her family. Includes fun facts and tips for training a cat to perform tricks.

ISBN 978-0-312-64121-4

[1. Cats—Fiction. 2. Babies—Fiction. 3. Adoption—Fiction.

4. Humorous stories.] I. Title.

PZ7.B82832Bam 2011 [E]—dc22

2010035699

ISBN 978-1-250-78236-6

Our books may be purchased in bulk for promotional, educational, or business use. Please contact your local bookseller or the Macmillan Corporate and Premium Sales Department at (800) 221-7945 ext. 5442 or by email at MacmillanSpecialMarkets@macmillan.com.

First edition, 2011 • Full-color edition, 2021

Book design by Aurora Parlagreco • Color by Saba Illustration

Printed in China by RR Donnelley Asia Printing Solutions Ltd.,

Dongguan City, Guangdong Province

1   3   5   7   9   10   8   6   4   2

• CONTENTS •

IN THE BEGINNING

IN THE BEGINNING, THERE WAS KITTY.

Just Kitty.

Only Kitty.

Kitty—all by herself.

And life was good.

Kitty ate her food—alone.

Kitty played with her toys—alone.

Kitty slept on the sofa—alone.

The years passed, and Kitty was happy to eat alone, play alone, and sleep alone. Life continued to be good—alone.

BUT ONE DAY . . .

. . . the skies became dark, the ground began to shake, the air became cold and dank and filled with a horrible stench.

A foul and wretched beast had arrived as if from nowhere.

Its face was deformed and grotesque. Its massive black nose was always cold and always wet. Its breath was so hot and so foul that its odor could mask the stench of a hundred dead fish lying in the sun. And it seemed to be filled with a noxious, clear liquid that continuously dripped out of the vast, gaping maw it called its mouth.

But what was worst of all, worse than its ugliness, worse than its terrible stink, and even worse than the never-ending trail of ooze it left behind wherever it went . . .

. . . was that the beast never seemed to sleep.

Kitty fought bravely to rid her once peaceful kingdom of the cruel beast. But even she wasn't mighty enough to defeat the evil creature.

Every time they confronted each other, the hideous beast would smear his foul, oily liquid on Kitty as if preparing to devour her.

Survival became a daily challenge for poor Kitty.

Over time, Kitty became used to life with the beast. Even its horrible odor became tolerable. The brave Kitty had found areas of shelter where she could evade the beast and its terrible liquid.

At times, though she would never admit it, she became almost fond of the beast.

Almost.

Life was not as it once was, but eventually it became good again.

Little did Kitty know that soon there would be another.

• CHAPTER ONE •
A SHORT TIME AWAY

GOOD MORNING, KITTY!

I suppose you're wondering why there are so many bags and suitcases on the floor.

Well, that's because we're going on a very special trip!

SPROING!

Uh . . . that is . . . WE are going on a very special trip. Sorry, Kitty, but you'll be staying here at home with Puppy.

DOUBLE FEH

Oh, don't be like that, Kitty. We won't be gone for long. And when we get back from our very special trip, we'll have a very special surprise for you.

So, Kitty, make sure that you listen to everything that Uncle Murray tells you. And make sure that you play nicely with Puppy. And make sure that you don't make a big mess while we're away.

29

UNCLE MURRAY'S FUN FACTS

'Cause they're out of their #@% mind That's why

WHY DO CATS CLIMB TREES?

All cats like to climb trees. Even big cats like lions and jaguars (but not most tigers) like to climb trees. And they all do it for three different reasons.

1) Cats like to climb trees . . . well . . . because they like to. Cats aren't very tall, so climbing up things like trees will give them the opportunity to see their surroundings from up high. Plus, while they're at it, climbing up a tree gives cats the opportunity to sharpen their claws, which they do all the time anyway.

And the higher up they go, the thinner the air, which is why they go #%&*@ crazy!

2) Cats will also climb trees because they're predators, which means that they hunt other animals. When they climb up a tree to inspect their surroundings, part of what they're looking for is something to eat. And as an added bonus, there happen to be some tasty things like birds and squirrels already nesting in those trees.

 Squirrels?! They eat squirrels?! Birds I knew about. But squirrels?! That's proof that cats are #%&*@ crazy!

3) Cats may be predators, but there are other bigger animals like dogs who sometimes attack cats. Climbing up a tree can often save a cat from harm.

Don't you believe it! That dog wouldn't hurt a fly!

33

Goodbye, Uncle Murray!

Hi, Kitty. Awww . . . You're not still sore at us for going on that trip without you, are you? Well, this will cheer you up! Do you remember that real big surprise we promised you? Do you? Do you?

AHEM... FEH

WELL, HERE SHE IS!

· CHAPTER TWO ·

WHAT THE HECK IS THAT THING?

41

PANIC, SINCE YOU CAME CLOSEST LAST WEEK WHEN YOU IDENTIFIED THE DUST BALL WE SAW UNDER THE SOFA AS "SOME SORT OF FUZZY COCKROACH MONSTER THAT WILL EAT US ALL," YOU GET TO BE THE FIRST TO PLAY **WHAT THE HECK IS THAT THING?**

Oh, wow! It's big. I mean, it's really big! And it drools a lot! I've never seen anything like it before! I should attack it. No, wait . . . I should run away! No, wait . . . I should attack it! No, wait . . .

PANIC

LAZY! LET'S HEAR WHAT YOU HAVE TO SAY!
WHAT THE HECK IS THAT THING?

47

49

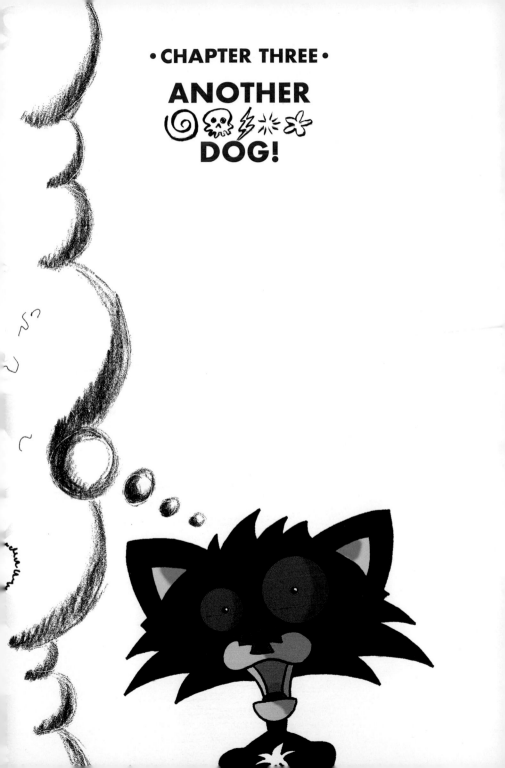

Oh, Kitty. Don't be like that. She's harmless. And the two of you have a lot in common. Really.

WHEEE!

GIGGLE

And just to prove it, I've invited all of your friends over to meet the newest addition to our family.

DING DONG!

Look, Kitty! It's all of the other kitties in the neighborhood! They'll prove to you that you have nothing to worry about!

*We would have been here sooner, but there was this really weird thing rolling around in the grass that could have been a snake or an armadillo or a hamburger wrapper, and we wanted to make sure that it wasn't a hamburger wrapper . . .

Awww! Isn't that sweet! They like her already. Now, aren't you ashamed of yourself, Kitty?

MEOW MEOW MEOW

so we all stopped to take turns sniffing it to make sure there wasn't any hamburger left in it and there wasn't, which was upsetting at first until we realized that at least it wasn't a snake or an armadillo, whatever that is.

Look! Big Kitty is noticing how big she is!

Awww! Isn't that sweet! Big Kitty must think she's another kitty!

The Twin Kitties are noticing how much she likes to play with their cat toys. They must think she's another kitty, too.

WHEE!

Stinky Kitty is noticing how . . . well . . . how stinky she can be. Stinky Kitty must think she's another kitty.

Chatty Kitty is noticing how talkative she is. Chatty Kitty must think she's another kitty.

*I like chicken. I like tuna. I like mackerel. I like . . .

Pretty Kitty is noticing how soft and delicate she is.
Pretty Kitty must think she's another kitty.

DOG

UNCLE MURRAY'S FUN FACTS

WHY DO CATS GET STUCK IN TREES?

Do we hav to do this now? I ju got home, and I'm tired!

If you look at a cat's claws close up, you'll see that they all curve inward toward their paws. This means that it's very easy for a cat to climb UP something, but not so easy for it to climb back DOWN unless the cat goes backward. That might sound easy enough for you or me, but moving backward does not come naturally to cats. Think about it this way . . . When was the last time you saw a cat walk backward?

I backed that goofy cat up against a wall a few days ago, and it was one of the worst experiences of my life!

So what sometimes happens is that when a kitten or a cat who's inexperienced with climbing goes up too high, she'll realize that it's too dangerous to jump down and simply won't know what to do. What's worse is that a frightened cat will often keep climbing higher and higher in the tree to find a different way down.

Which is not at all like what happened to me when I got stuck in the tree. See, I kept climbing up and up thinking that the higher you get in the tree, the longer the branches get. And eventually I'd find a branch long enough to get me back down. Makes sense, right?

69

The athletes are entering the room! And what a colorful group they are!

 I know I say this every time, S.K., but this is always my favorite part of these games.

 Here comes Big Kitty! You can tell that he's been training.

The Twin Kitties look eager to compete. True champions, the both of them.

Pretty Kitty is looking as lovely as ever! *sigh*

And just behind her, Stinky Kitty is looking as filthy as ever! *Ack!*

Here comes Chatty Kitty, trying to psyche out the competition as usual.

And here comes our host kitty! Wow! I don't know if I've ever seen such a look of determination on an athlete's face. This could mean trouble!

MEOW MEOW*

*Did you know that the first parade was really just a bunch of rocks that were all rolling down a hill at the same time and fell into a tuba? It's true! I looked it up.

And following her is the New Kitty. What do you think we can expect from this newcomer?

Hard to say, S.K. She's a plucky, young go-getter with a will to win. That much is for sure.

This could get exciting, folks! LET THE GAMES BEGIN!

This first event is always a crowd pleaser! It's the STARE-AT-YOURSELF-IN-A-MIRROR-UNTIL-YOU-GET-BORED competition. Pretty Kitty remains undefeated in this event, but Stinky Kitty has promised to give her a challenge.

Pretty Kitty's looking good, S.K.
And I mean very, VERY good. *sigh*
Couldn't you just swim in those big,
dark, beautiful eyes? And her fur—
so soft . . . so velvety . . .

 Sorry to interrupt, but something
is happening out on the floor!

ZZZZZ

ABA
AGA

Stinky Kitty is asleep! I think he's always been asleep! That means he's automatically disqualified! And that means this contest is just between . . .

Hold that thought, S.K.! Something else is happening!

ZZZZZ

Oooo!

WOW! Pretty Kitty was momentarily distracted! And that means that in a stunning upset, the NEW KITTY IS THE WINNER!

YOP!

ZZZZ

79

The BABBLING-ON-AND-ON-WITHOUT-STOPPING event has been Chatty Kitty's domain for many years now. But Big Kitty is hoping for an upset today. And apparently so is our ambitious young newcomer, fresh from her recent victory. Let's watch the action!

MEOW MEOW!

MEOW MEOW MEOW MEOW*

BA BA BA BA BA

*I was watching television last week when someone—I think he was either an actor or a doctor or an actor who plays a doctor on a TV show or a doctor who plays an actor on a TV show, but that doesn't make any sense—said that eggs were good for a cat's fur, which sounded just gross because I think your fur would get all sticky and weird if you rubbed eggs on yourself.

This could go on for hours, folks. So feel free to step into another room to get a drink of water or find some cotton for your ears or . . .

MEOW!

MEOW MEOW MEOW MEOW*

BA BA BA BA BA

*He might have meant that you had to cook the eggs first, but how would you cook them? It might feel nice if you scrambled them, but that could still get messy, and hard-boiled eggs would feel kind of odd even if you peeled them. I think fried eggs would be the kind of eggs I would put on my fur because they would probably stick there the longest until, of course, it rained and then I would . . .

Big Kitty and Chatty Kitty have both been left speechless! Speechless! What a stunning victory for New Kitty!

BA
BA
BA
WHEEE!

Well, folks, despite protests from the neighbors, it's time once again for the WHO-CAN-CREATE-THE-BIGGEST-STINK event, also known as the WHO-CAN-OUTSTINK-STINKY-KITTY competition. This is a grueling event that's not for the faint of heart.

The Twin Kitties took up the challenge this year. Rumor has it that they rolled around in the dumpster behind a seafood restaurant and bathed in garlic juice just before the event.

But, as expected, even the Twin Kitties look overcome by the inspiringly putrid essence of Stinky Kitty. This event is just about over.

But wait! New Kitty is entering the playing field! Could this amazing athlete really pose a challenge to Stinky Kitty?

What could she possibly do this late in the game? What could she possibly do that could emit such a noxious odor big enough to . . .

NNNNNNG...

What an amazing athlete! What an amazing kitty! What a true champion! What a stunning defeat for Stinky Kitty! A new era has come! This day will go down in history!

FLOP!

WHEW! I think it's time to change your diaper, young lady. And then we'll get you something to eat.

And no other kitty in the history of The Pussycat Olympics has ever dominated this sport more than our host. Time and time again, she has consumed more food than could ever be imagined. Time and time again, she has proved that no meal is too large, no food bowl too deep, no menu too absurd for this kitty and her extraordinary appetite.

SUPPER TIME, KITTY!

Is there no one brave enough, heroic enough, hungry enough to challenge the champion? Is there no courageous kitty out there who is willing to test her appetite and her stomach against the master's? No one? Really? No one?

Okay, athletes! You know the rules! Whoever finishes her bowl of food first wins!

ON YOUR MARK . . .

GET SET . . .

GO!

YUM!

KITTY

101

WHAT AN INCREDIBLE PERFORMANCE! NEW KITTY HAS DONE THE IMPOSSIBLE AND WON EVERY SINGLE EVENT IN THE PUSSYCAT OLYMPICS!

She's more than just a kitty, she's a SUPER KITTY!

BO!

Tell us . . . now that you've <u>LOST</u>, can you tell our audience how it feels to have <u>LOST</u> because this is the first time you've ever <u>LOST</u> this event. Plus, you <u>LOST</u> to a newcomer.

109

One more event has been added to the schedule, folks—the 20-FOOT-CAT-SPRINT-OUT-THE-DOOR! Anyone who makes it back home in one piece is a winner!

*Look out! Gangway! Move it or lose it!

111

• CHAPTER FIVE •

OUR REGULARLY SCHEDULED SCREAMING TEMPER TANTRUM

Well, Kitty . . . You've done it again. Everyone was having such a nice time until you had to go and spoil it by freaking out. And why? Because you lost a few little games.

We love you, Kitty, but sometimes you're not just a **Bad Kitty**. Sometimes you're a bad loser, too.

TSK
TSK
TSK

No, Kitty. It's not her fault. It's nobody's fault but your own.

Now where do you think you're going?

BUHBYE!

SNORT

No, Kitty. She's not moving out. She's staying here with us whether you like it or not.

OOOH!

Sigh No, Kitty. We can't ship her back to where she came from.

BOK!

THIS END UP

117

No, Kitty. We're not going to sell her either. Now stop it!

That's right, Kitty. This baby needed someone to feed her. This baby needed someone to read her stories and play with her. This baby needed someone to love her and take good care of her— just like you and Puppy once needed all of those things.

BLEH!

FOR SALE
ONLY 20¢ 10¢ 5¢

FREE DOG WITH EVERY PURCHASE

And this baby needed a place to live that was warm and safe and happy just like you and Puppy once needed this place.

BAH!

FREE DOG
WITH EVERY
PURCHASE

This baby needed a home just like you and Puppy once needed a home. And now she has all that . . .

FREE DOG
WITH EVERY
PURCHASE

Never mind.

UNCLE MURRAY'S FUN FACTS

You don't! Life's too short!

HOW DO YOU GET A CAT BACK DOWN FROM A TREE?

In most cases, a cat stuck in a tree will find a way down all by herself once she figures out how to shimmy back down backward. But there are some techniques you can use to help her.

1) Open a can of her favorite food underneath the tree. Make sure, if possible, that she sees it and then leave it at the bottom of the tree. Nothing will convince your cat to take a risk like a hungry stomach.

2) If you have a ladder tall enough to reach the cat or even come a little close, then prop it up securely against the tree and let her climb down by herself.

3) Leave her alone or at least walk away from the tree. Sometimes even your best intentions might make your cat even more nervous during this awful experience. Letting her find the food or the ladder by herself could be the best tactic.

But if hours pass or it's starting to get dark or cold outside, then it might be time to take matters into your own hands. If the cat isn't too high up and if your ladder is sturdy enough, put on a thick coat and a pair of thick work gloves and go on up to get her. Move slowly so you don't make her more nervous. Try to grab her by the scruff of the neck. Even though cats hate this, you'll need your other hand to climb back down.

If the situation becomes a real emergency or if the cat is just too high up to reach by yourself, avoid calling the fire department if at all possible. Despite their reputation, many fire departments have a strict policy against cat rescues. This is because the time spent rescuing a cat from a tree could distract them from a fire that could be taking place elsewhere.

Instead, call your local animal shelter or humane society. They're the real professionals for this sort of thing.

Great. Now you tell me.

131

•CHAPTER SIX•
A NEW BEGINNING

Well, Kitty. I guess it's nice that you've become so close to the baby.

But sometimes . . .

No, Kitty! The baby doesn't use the litter box like you. That's why she wears a diaper.

No, Kitty! The baby doesn't eat cat food like you.
That's why we feed her apples and bananas and
cereal.

HUH?

No, Kitty! The baby doesn't play with fuzzy toy mice like you. That's why we give her blocks and cars and teething rings.

HUH?

No, Kitty! You don't need to lick the baby clean like you clean yourself. That's why we give her a <u>BATH</u>.

GIGGLE!

That's right, Kitty. Babies get BATHS. Babies like BATHS. In fact, now that this baby is all covered in cat litter, cat food, fuzz, and your slobber, it's time that we gave her a . . .

BATH!

Oh, Kitty. Don't be like that. She likes baths. Really. It's true. Don't you believe me?

What are you doing, Kitty? Are you going to help me take the baby to the bathtub? Are you going to help me give her a bath? Kitty?

Kitty . . . ?

• APPENDIX •
CAT TRICKS

During The Pussycat Olympics, we saw all of the kitties compete in some fairly basic feline activities like meowing and eating. But cats are capable of performing some great feats, even though dogs are usually the ones with the reputation for executing tricks.

The one thing you'll need to get tricks is to bring treats. Keep a little cat kibble around for training your cat because you'll need them to reward her when she does what you want.

COME: This one should be easy. Every time you feed your cat, call to her with the same word such as "come" or "here." Trainers call this a "cue word." Eventually, the cat will come to you every time you use that word. Reward her with a treat when she does.

SIT: Hold a treat to your cat's nose. When she becomes interested, move the treat up over her head until she naturally takes a sitting position. When she sits down, give her the treat. After you've been able to do this several times, introduce the cue word of "sit" into her training. After a while, she should be able to sit on command.

SHAKE A PAW: Once you have been able to teach your cat to sit, try gently tapping her front paw while saying "shake." Once she naturally lifts her paw up, gently take it into your hand and then give her a treat.

SITTING UP OR BEGGING: Once your cat has mastered sitting, try holding a treat up a little higher than usual. It will take several tries, but once your cat lifts her front paws off the ground, give her the treat right away. Over time, you can lift the treat higher so the cat has to reach higher. Eventually you may be able to train your cat to sit or even stand up on hind legs alone on command.

When you train your cat, you have to remember two things: BE PATIENT because, depending on the cat, even the simplest tricks can take several days, weeks, or even months to learn. And DON'T OVERFEED YOUR CAT. Tricks are fun to teach your cat, but not at the expense of making her too fat because of all the rewards you're giving her.

TACO, PLEASE!

143

• ABOUT THE AUTHOR •

NICK BRUEL is the author and illustrator of the phenomenally successful Bad Kitty series, including *Bad Kitty Meets the Baby* and *Bad Kitty for President*. Nick has also written and illustrated popular picture books, including *A Wonderful Year* and his most recent, *Bad Kitty: Searching for Santa*. Nick lives with his wife and daughter in Westchester, New York. Visit him at **nickbruelbooks.com**.